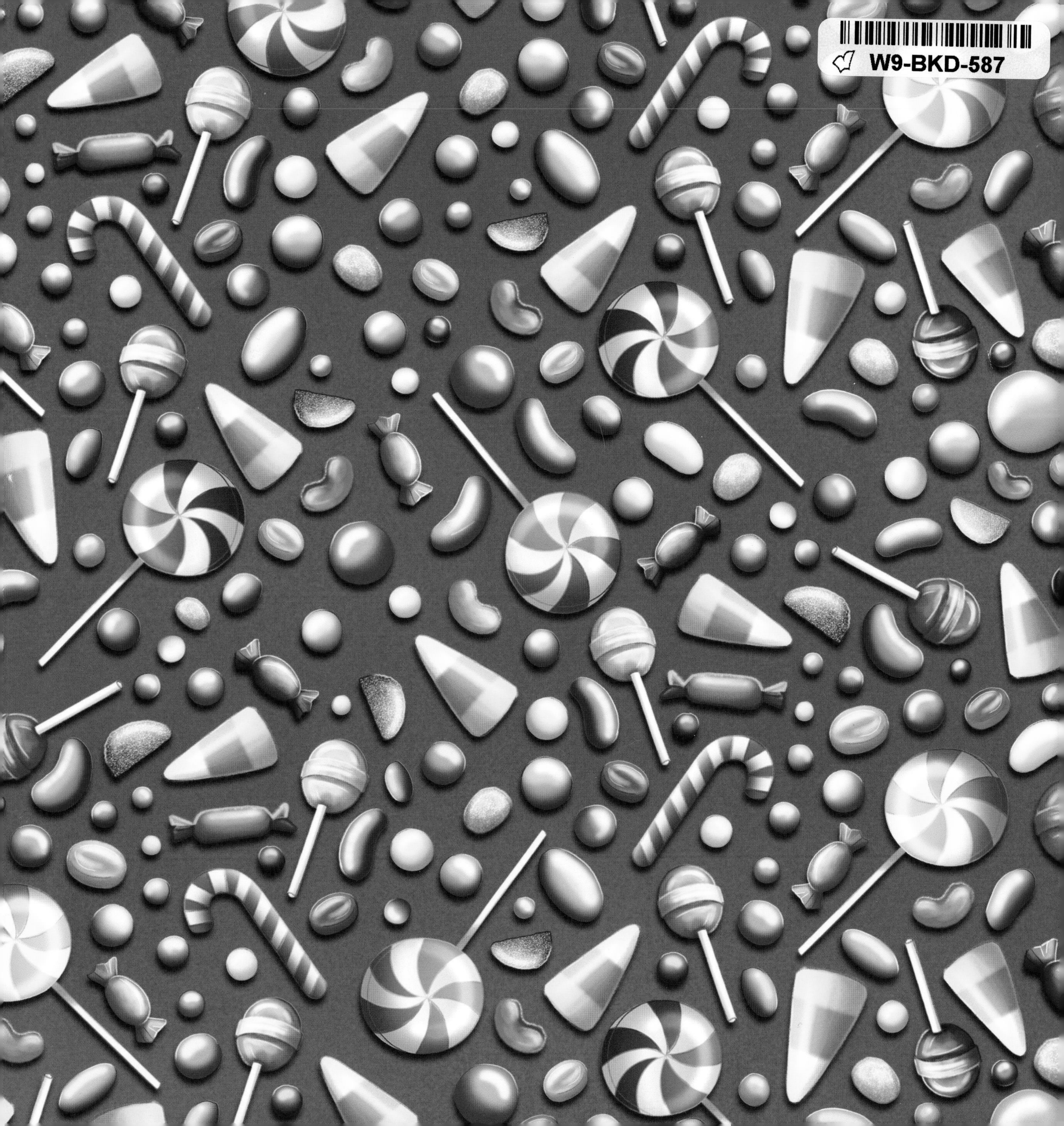

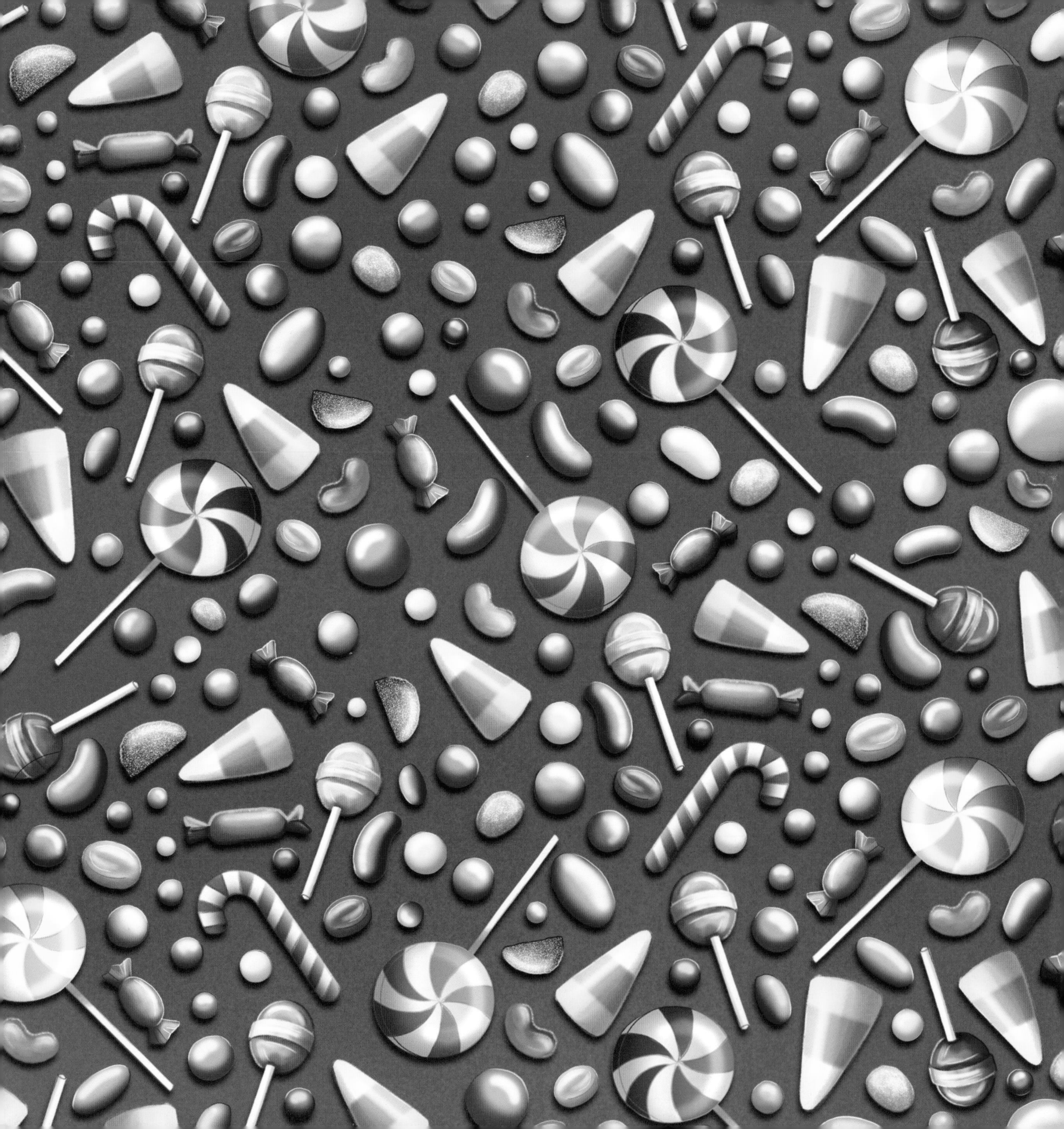

The Three Little

# SUPERPIGS

## TRICK OR TREAT?

**For Joe, Amy, and Max. X**



Library of Congress Cataloging-in-Publication Data available.

ISBN 978-1-338-77063-6

10 9 8 7 6 5 4 3 21 22 23 24 25

Printed in the U.S.A. 76

First edition, July 2021

# The Three Little SUPERPIGS

## TRICK OR TREAT?

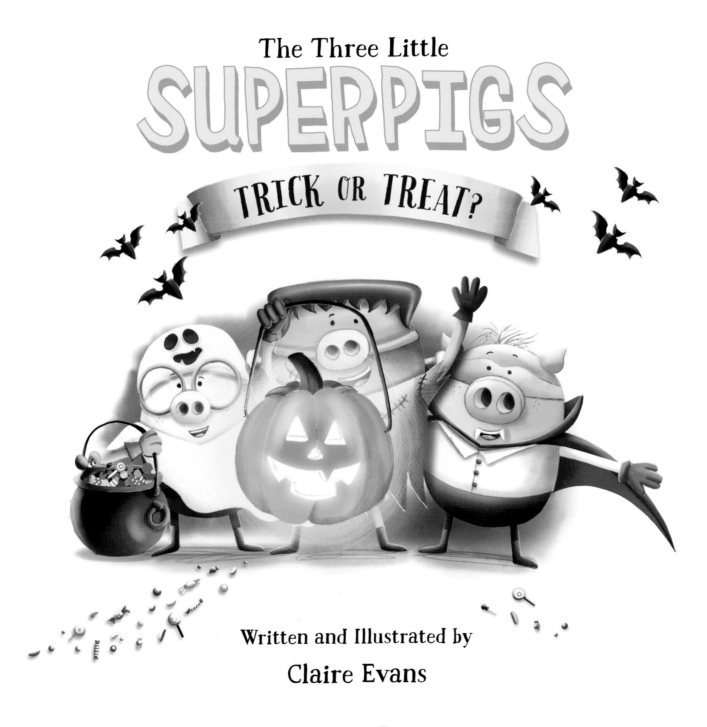

Written and Illustrated by

Claire Evans

Scholastic Press
New York

It was the morning of Halloween,
and all of Fairyland was excited.

The SUPERPIGS had been invited to perform at the annual Spooktacular Halloween Parade as Fairyland's very special guests.

But they had two hair-raising problems: What should they perform, and what costumes should they wear?

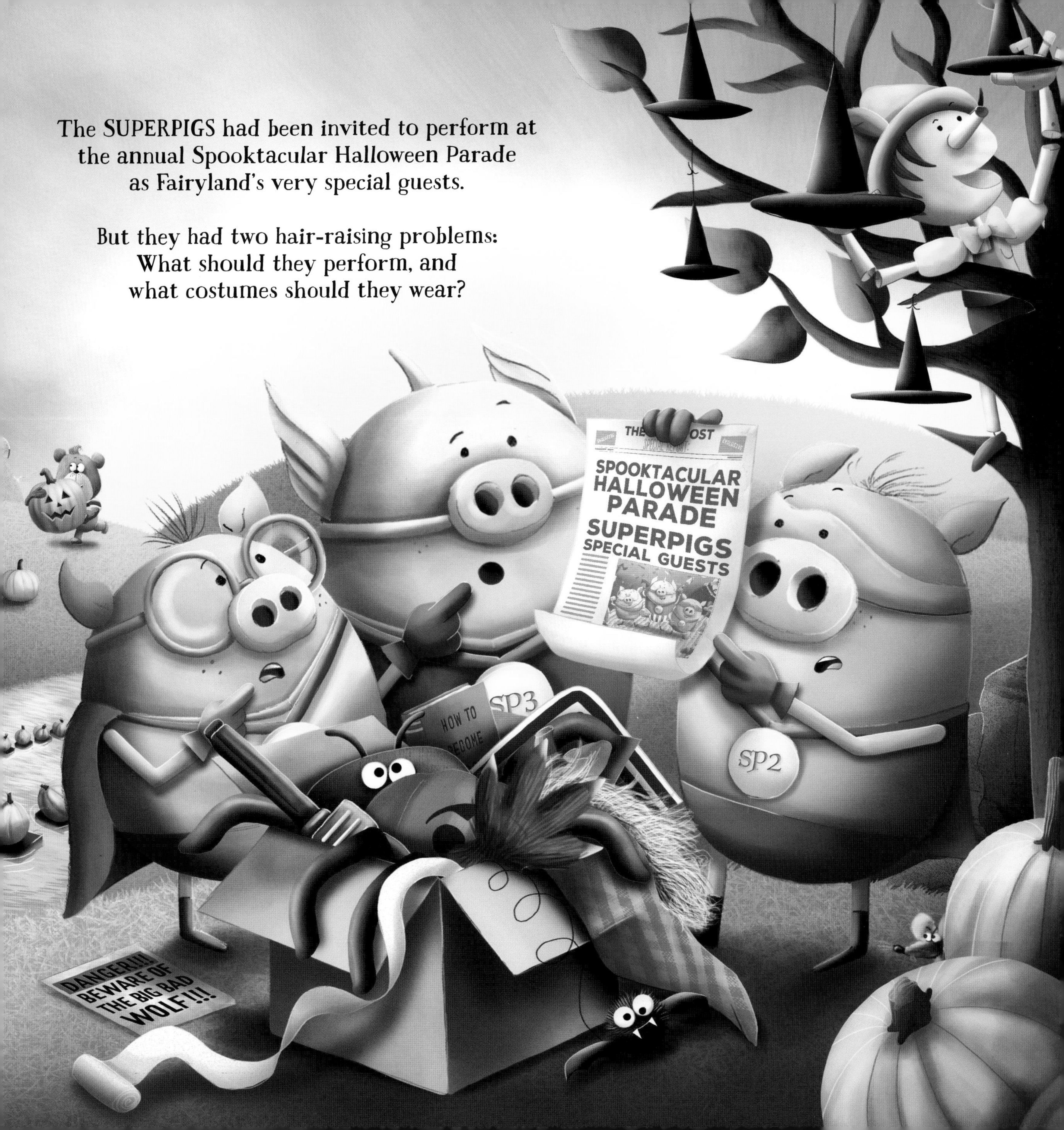

The first SUPERPIG tried on
one costume, but it kept unraveling.

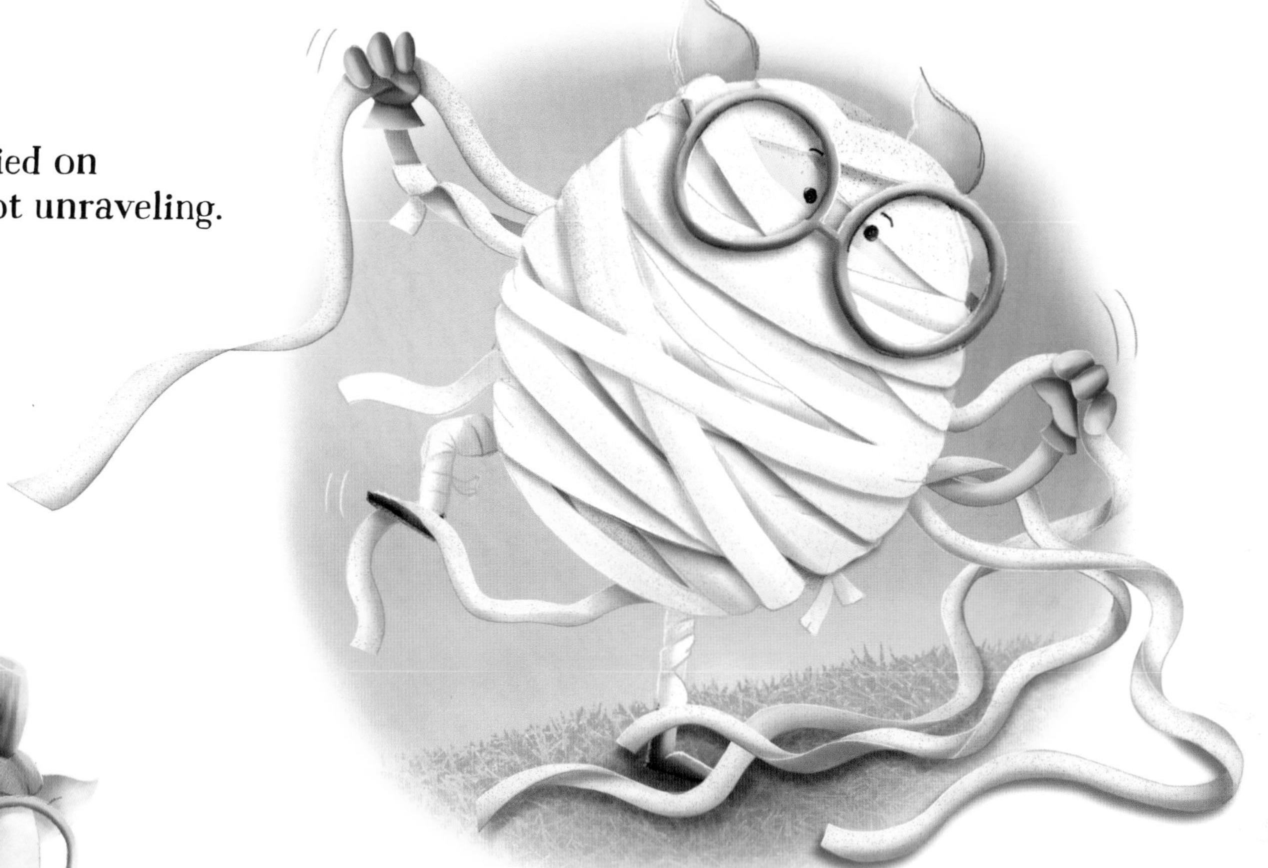

Then he tried on his second costume,
but he kept toppling over.

Finally, he tried on a ghost costume. "I can practice my super-speed in this and run so fast, I'll be invisible!" he said.

The second SUPERPIG tried on his first costume, but he kept getting tangled in all the legs!

Then he tried on his second costume, but it reminded him too much of somebody they knew.

Finally, he tried on a vampire costume.
"I can fly through the air with ease in this!"
he declared.

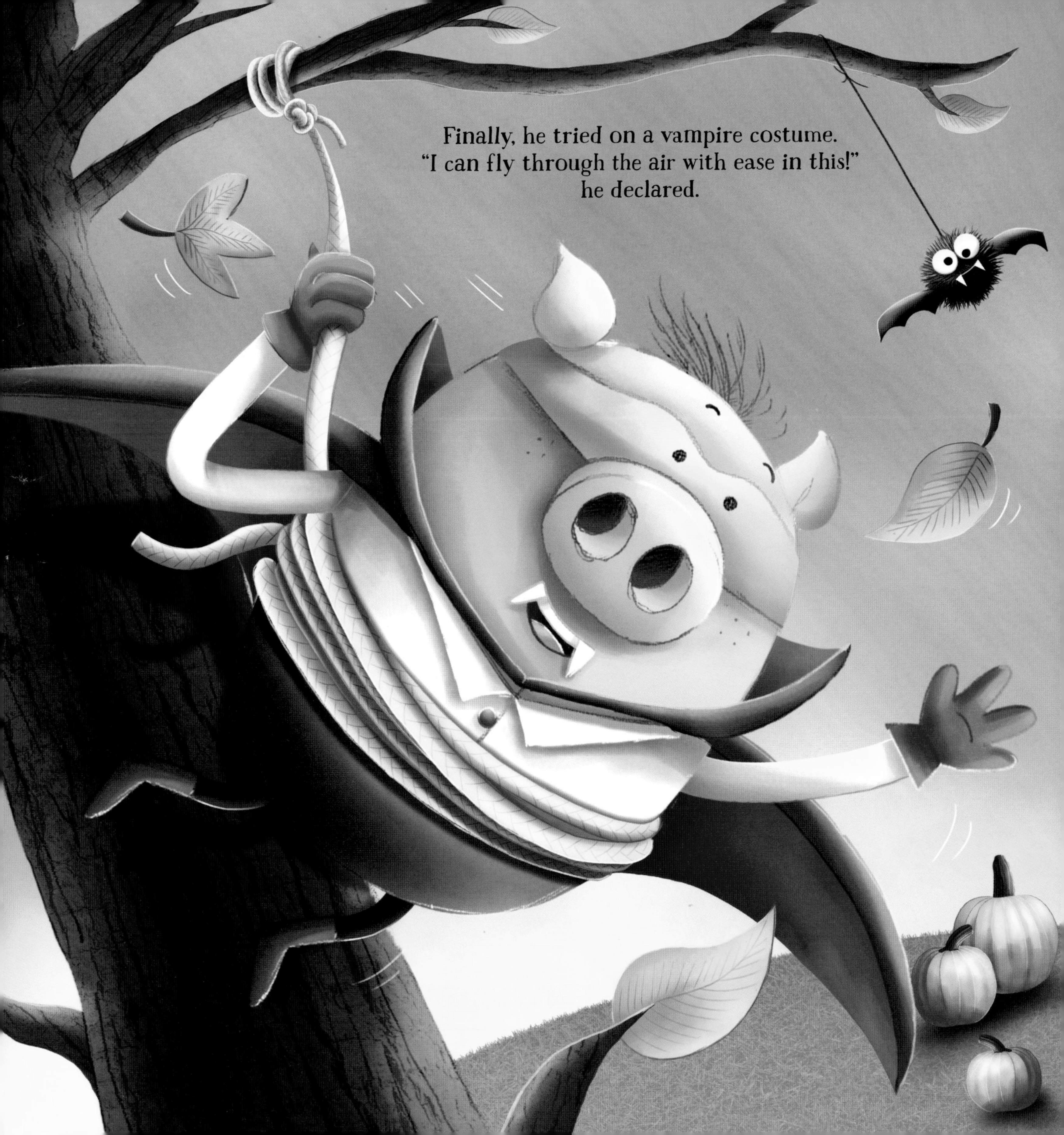

The third SUPERPIG tried on his
first costume, but the wig
kept getting in his eyes
and he couldn't see!

Then he tried on his second
costume, but the backpack
was too heavy.

Finally, he tried on a monster costume. "I can lift everything with monstrous ease now! I'll work on my super-strength!" he decided.

But even in their
super-duper costumes,
the Superpigs still couldn't figure out
what to do for their Spooktacular
Halloween Parade routine.

But they knew if they kept trying,
they'd work it out.
"Practice makes perfect!"
they reminded themselves.

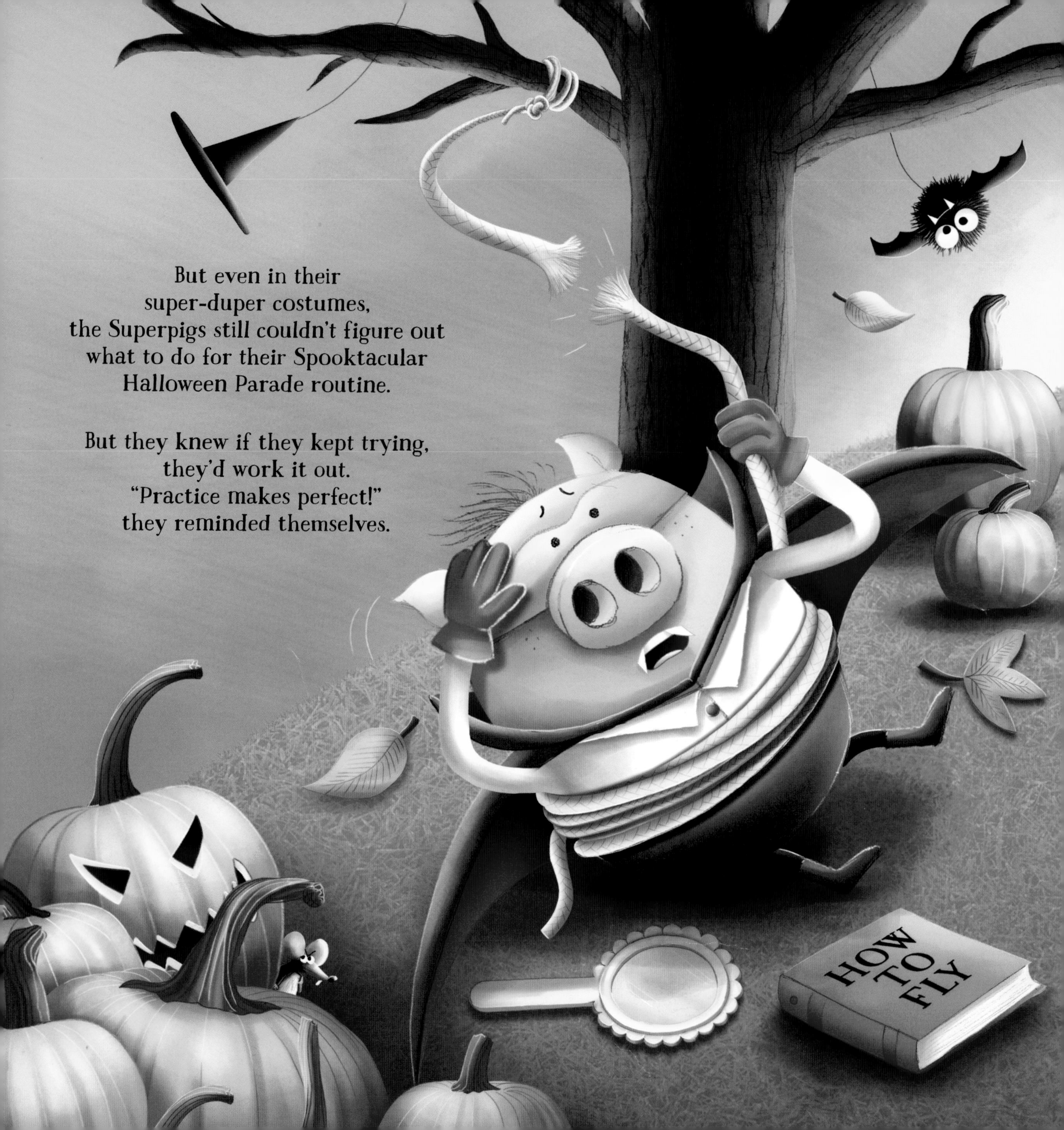

HOW TO BECOME STRONG

DANGER!!!
BEWARE OF
THE WICKED
WITCH!!

Suddenly, Hansel and Gretel arrived.
They looked spooked!
"The Wicked Witch has stolen all the
Halloween candy for the parade!"
they told the Superpigs.

"She lives in the Deep Dark Woods and has taken all of the candy to decorate her gingerbread house!" Hansel and Gretel explained.

"We have to stop the Wicked Witch and save Halloween!" the SUPERPIGS declared.

In pursuit, they spotted
something shiny.
It was a trail of
delicious candy!

"It looks like the naughty Witch
has dropped some of the
Halloween candy she stole!"
said the SUPERPIGS.
"Follow that trail!"

DANGER!!!
BEWARE OF
THE WICKED
WITCH!!

The Superpigs followed the trail of treats,
crossing dangerous ravines and scaling crumbling cliffs.

Collecting candy as evidence
the whole way, they finally found . . .

. . . the gingerbread house!
"Just like Hansel and Gretel said,"
gasped the Superpigs.
"And it's covered in the
stolen candy!"

After sampling some candy "evidence,"
the pigs crept inside the house
to catch the Wicked Witch.

But instead, they were greeted
with a terrible surprise!

"TRICK OR TREAT?!" shouted a familiar voice.

It was THE BIG BAD WOLF!
"Gotcha!" he jeered
as he captured the pigs
in his trusty net.

"Hahaha! So glad you finally got here,
but the WITCH was not the one to fear!"
the Wolf laughed.

"I gobbled her up . . .

. . . but my tummy got sore!

So I spat her back out and she ran for the door!"
the Wolf cackled.

"Now I'm still hungry
and ready to eat
the Three Little SUPERPIGS —
Oh, what a TREAT!"

Pointing to a mop and bucket in the corner of the room, the Wolf ordered the ghostly SUPERPIG to scrub the floor. He wanted the house clean and tidy in time for his delicious feast.

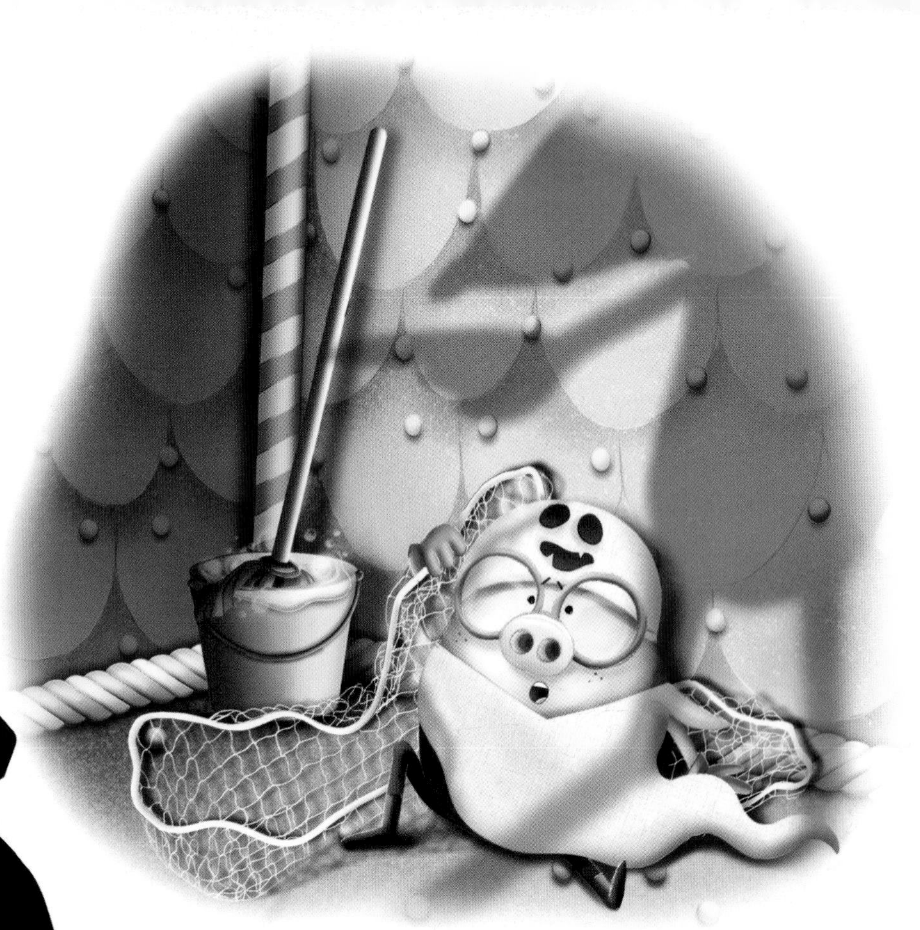

"Well, I'm not waiting any longer. These hunger pangs are getting stronger!" he growled impatiently as he lit the fire.

"Now, who should I cook first?" he smirked.

"Not so fast, BIG BAD WOLF!" cried the ghostly SUPERPIG.

Using his super-speed, he shot across the room and doused the Wolf in slimy, soapy water. The Wolf was stunned! Meanwhile monster SUPERPIG used his super-strength to pry open the bars of the steel cage.

Using his cape, the vampire SUPERPIG flew out of the cage and landed a direct hit.

The nasty villain slid straight across the slippery wet floor,

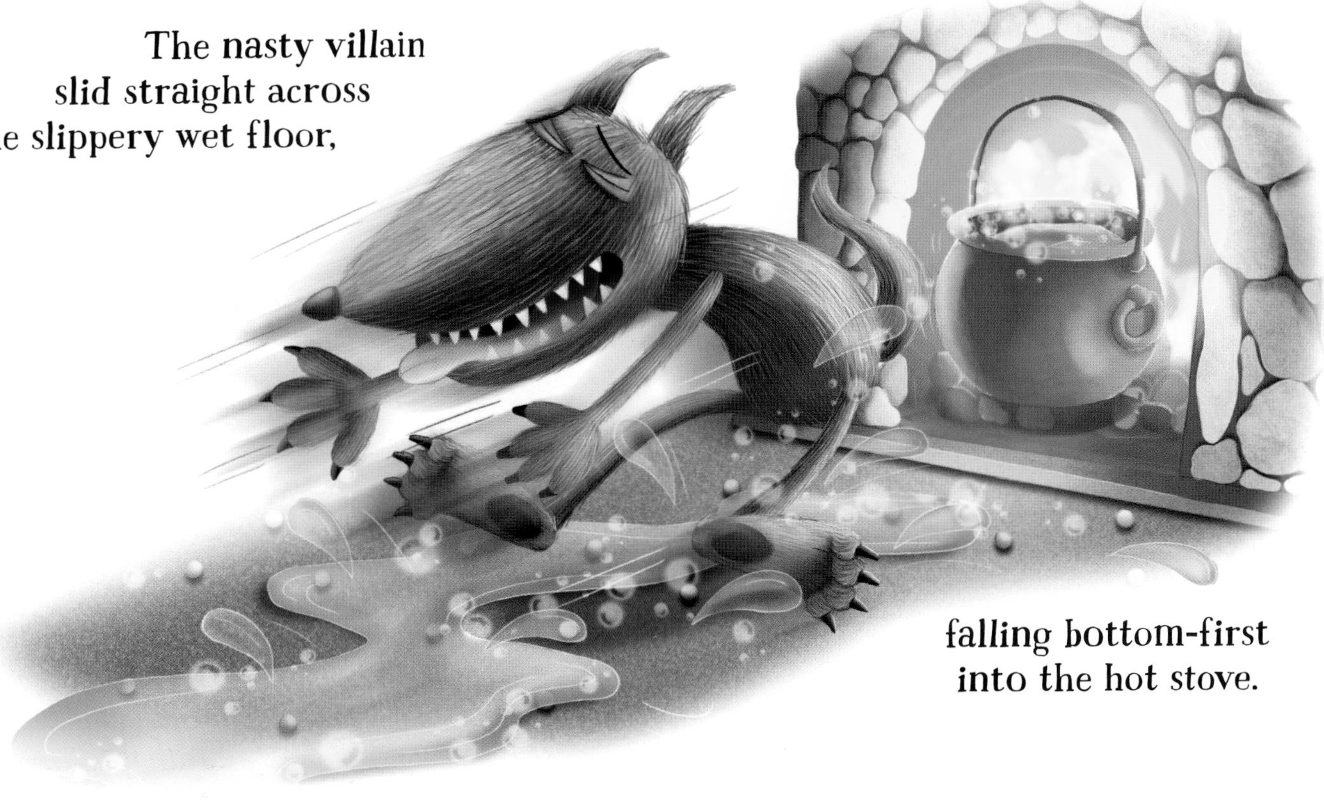

falling bottom-first into the hot stove.

"OWWWWWWW!!!"

howled the Wolf as he jumped
out of the furnace
and fled the house,
followed by a trail of smoke.

The three SUPERPIGS had defeated the nasty Wolf once again using their SUPER SKILLS.

"Practice really does make perfect!" they all agreed.

The Wicked Witch came out of hiding and thanked the SUPERPIGS for defeating the BIG BAD WOLF.

"I'll never steal Fairyland's Halloween candy ever again!" she promised.

The Wicked Witch gave back all the stolen candy and allowed the SUPERPIGS to ride her magic broomstick back to Fairyland. It was almost time for the Spooktacular Halloween Parade!

The pigs said
goodbye
and zoomed
off into
the night sky!

The SUPERPIGS arrived just in time to perfectly perform their impressive new flying routine, and they gave out Halloween TREATS to all the people of Fairyland.

It was the best Spooktacular
Halloween Parade ever!
The whole town cheered:

"Hooray for the
three little SUPERPIGS!
Happy Halloween!"

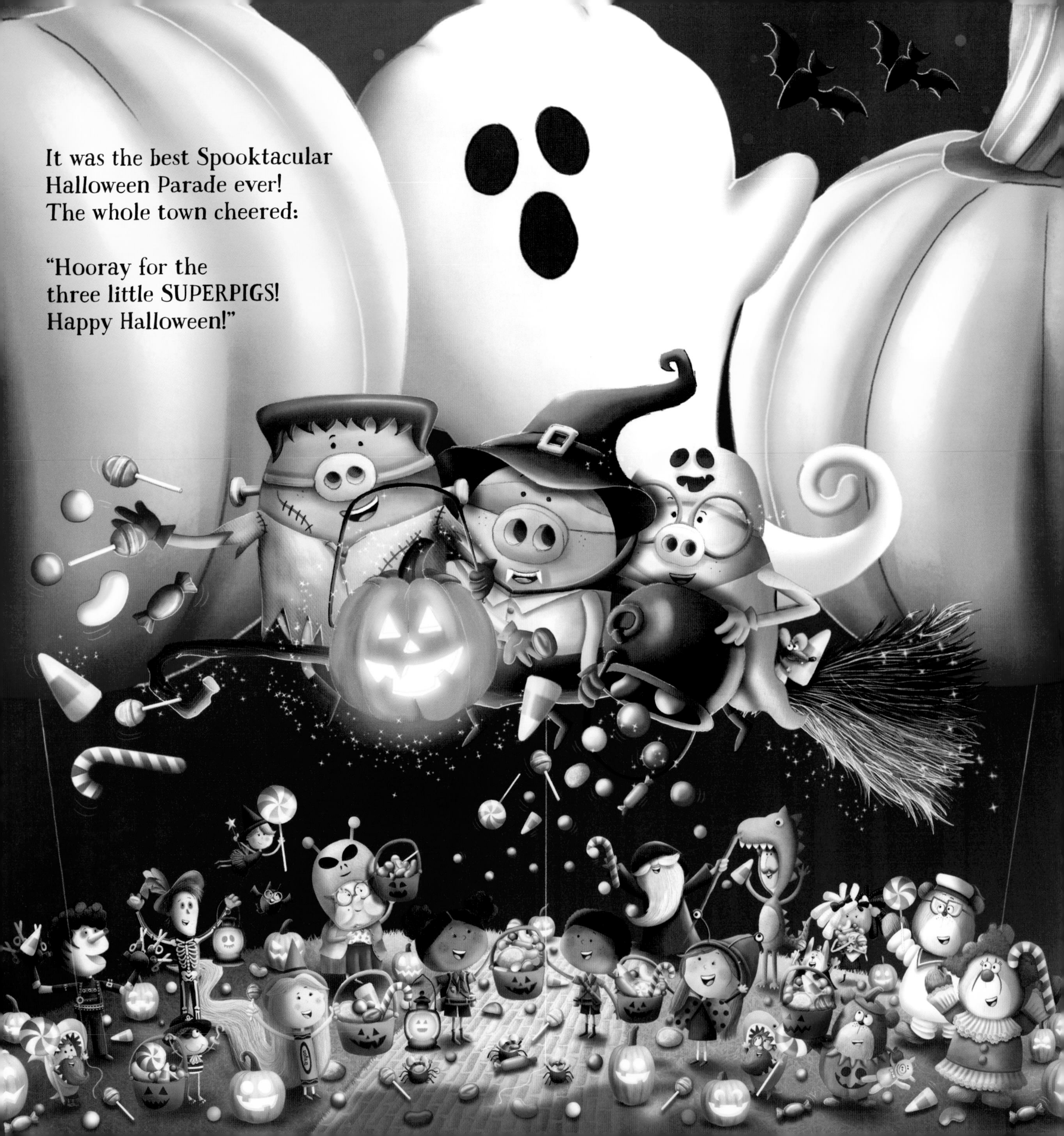

The end?